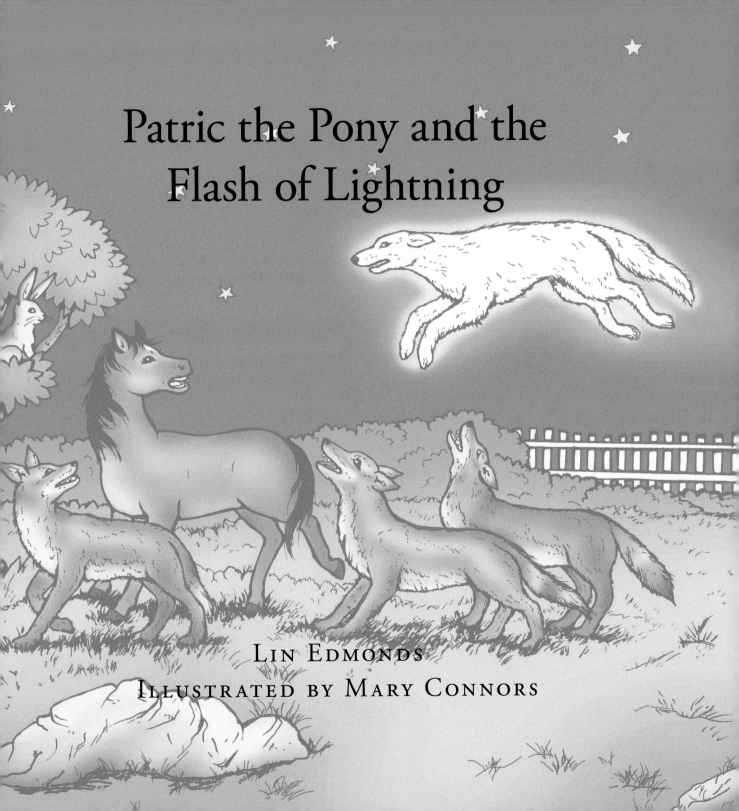

Patric the Pony and the Flash of Lightning

LIN EDMONDS

ILLUSTRATED BY MARY CONNORS

AuthorHouse™
1663 Liberty Drive
Bloomington, IN 47403
www.authorhouse.com
Phone: 833-262-8899

Because of the dynamic nature of the Internet, any web addresses or links contained in this book may have changed
since publication and may no longer be valid. The views expressed in this work are solely those of the author and do not
necessarily reflect the views of the publisher, and the publisher hereby disclaims any responsibility for them.

Any people depicted in stock imagery provided by Getty Images are models,
and such images are being used for illustrative purposes only.
Certain stock imagery © Getty Images.

This book is printed on acid-free paper.

ISBN: 978-1-4389-6302-0 (sc)

Print information available on the last page.

Published by AuthorHouse 08/27/2022

authorHOUSE®

The days were cold and frosty. Patric's brown coat had grown thick and long to keep him warm. There were very few flies for the frog to eat, and one day the frog told the pony that it was time for him to sleep until spring.

"Goodnight, Patric," he said. "See you next year," and he hopped into his burrow beside the pond where it was warm and dry.

"Sleep well Froggy," said Patric. "See you next year."

The grass was dry and brown and tired, and there was no more goodness in it. Olivia and little Jacob walked down the hill twice a day to feed Patric. The rabbit was hungry. "Come and have some hay," said Patric. The rabbit was happy to share Patric's hay, and the two friends ate together every day.

It was almost the shortest day of the year and the longest night. The moon was full and bright, and Patric could see its reflection in the water of the pond. He could hear the coyotes singing a hunting song to the moon. Yip, yip, yip," they sang. It was so cold Patric could see his breath hanging in the still air. He dipped his nose into the water and drank, and then he sighed. He missed his friend the frog, he missed the fresh, green grass.

Suddenly, there was movement. Startled, he raised his head. In the moonlight, he saw Harry the rabbit running toward him from the marshy ground at the far end of the meadow.

"Run, run for your life," said Harry as he ran by. "They found me. They're coming," and away he ran up the hill.

Who found you? wondered Patric as he followed Harry as fast as he could. "Who is coming?" he asked the rabbit as they ran, but all the rabbit could say was, "Faster, Patric, faster."

When he reached the top of the hill, Patric could see Harry running up and down in front of the fence. To Harry the fence looked as if it reached up to the sky. "No way out, no way out. What shall I do, what shall I do?" he cried. "They will eat me; this time they will eat me!"

Patric jumped on top of the big, flat rock and looked down the hill. It was then that he saw them in the moonlight. Narrow, dark shadows with long legs trotting up the hill toward them. Coyotes! The coyotes were coming.

Patric looked around. How could he help his friend? Then he jumped down from the rock and trotted over to the big oak tree. It was green, with wide, spreading branches. "Here, rabbit," he said.

"Jump on my back and then onto that low branch. You'll be safe in the tree," and he dropped down to his knees.

Harry the rabbit jumped onto Patric's back. Patric stood up, and then Harry jumped onto the branch in the oak tree. He scrambled to the highest place on the branch, and he hid among the leaves. He tucked his nose in between his paws and folded his ears against his sides, and he pretended he wasn't there at all.

"Don't move until I tell you it's okay," whispered Patric.

Patric moved away from the tree and looked around him. Where were the coyotes? All was quiet. There was no wind and only a few clouds in the sky. Perhaps the coyotes have gone away, he thought hopefully. Suddenly he smelled something. Something in the shadow of the rock was watching him. They were here!

Long-legged and thin in the body, the pack leader trotted boldly out into the moonlight. Its large ears stood straight up on its head. Its eyes were yellow slits. It trotted lightly around Patric and around the tree, stopping every now and to scratch its belly. It sniffed the ground with its long nose. It sniffed the air. Then it sat in front of Patric and said in a singsong voice, "We're looking for a rabbit. We are friends of his. We know his family well. Is he in this tree?" Then it stood on its hind legs under the very branch where Harry was hiding, and it sniffed and sniffed the cold air. It could almost reach the branch. Its eyes were here and its eyes were there, and Patric thought they saw everything. "Yes, I can smell the rabbit. He is in this tree," the coyote sang out.

"Yip, yip, yip," sang the rest of the pack from the shadow of the rock. "Yip, yip, yip, the rabbit is in the tree."

Patric could see their eyes glowing in the darkness. He knew the coyote was not the rabbit's friend, and there was something about the coyote that made him feel afraid. All the hairs in his mane prickled and stood on end. What was happening?

Quickly, Patric stood under the branch were Harry was hiding. Again the leader of the coyotes sat in front of him. This time it stretched very tall and raised its head and yawned very slowly, showing all of its long, sharp, white teeth. Then it said, "We were thinking of playing a game with the rabbit. But what is one rabbit between friends? Let's share the rabbit. Move away from the tree!"

Share the rabbit with him, what does that mean? Patric wondered for a moment. Then he knew what the coyote meant, and he did not move away from the tree.

"So be it," said the coyote leader very softly. "I am so happy to meet you, pony. What a handsome pony you are. We are many, and after all, a rabbit is very small."

Then he got up and trotted around Patric. Patric saw that saliva was dripping from the coyote's mouth. Suddenly he grew very, very afraid. Patric was afraid from the tip of his nose down to the heels of his small, hard hooves. He turned, and as he turned he saw that there were coyotes all around him. He wanted to run and run and run, but there was no way out. There was nowhere to hide. He knew now why the coyotes made him feel afraid. They wanted to eat him too!

The rest of the coyote pack trotted out from behind the rock, and when Patric saw them coming toward him, he raised himself up very tall and pinned back his ears. Then swiftly he turned around and backed toward them, kicking. Surprised, they scattered out of the way. But this was a game they had played many times before, and they circled him quickly and leaped for his throat. They leaped and bit at his sides. They circled and bit at his hind legs with their long, sharp teeth.

Patric screamed with pain and plunged and reared. He kicked and kicked at them with his hard hooves until they howled and slunk away into the darkness, but out of the shadows came more coyotes, and they attacked him again. They bit at his flanks and his hind legs, and again and again the pack leader leaped for his throat, trying to pull him down. What was happening? What could he do? He wanted to run and run, but he knew he must not leave Harry.

He bit hard with his teeth and kicked hard with his hooves until the coyotes whimpered, but they were many and they were hungry. Patric grew tired and afraid for himself and for Harry. Patric was a Mountain pony, and he had raced many times around the meadow with Harry the rabbit. He was strong and tough, and he was agile, but he wondered how long he could hold out against so many determined attackers? Desperately, he kept on fighting, pushing the coyotes back away from the tree, but he was tired and he was weakening.

The coyote leader saw that that he was weakening and urged on the pack. "Soon, soon, the pony is ours," he howled.

Then suddenly, from over the fence that ran from one end of the meadow to the other, out of the corner of one eye, Patric glimpsed a large, white shape. Is it a ghost? he wondered. The coyotes saw the strange white shape too, and they stopped to watch. All the hair on their backs stood on end, and they growled. What was it? It had a long, white, flowing coat and a long, long tail. It seemed to float over the ground toward them at great speed.

It cried out, "Make way, make way for Éclair the borzoi. Beware, coyotes, beware!" Into the moonlight leaped a large white dog. Before they could move, she charged the coyotes with swiftly snapping teeth.

Éclair was here, she was there; her teeth were everywhere. The coyote pack scattered, yipping with surprise. Patric saw the coyote leader reach up into the tree, into the very branch where the rabbit was hiding. He called out to the white dog, "Quick, we must get to the tree." Éclair ran to the tree, reached over the back of the coyote leader, grabbed him by the neck, lifted him off the ground, and shook him. The coyote howled with fear and twisted and snapped his teeth as he was shaken and shaken and shaken and then thrown to the ground.

Éclair held him down by the neck so that he could not move and whispered in his ear, "Leave, leave his place… Or else!" The coyote leader lay still as he was released and lay as if he were dead. Then he staggered to his feet and began to slink away down the hill. Then all the coyotes were afraid, and they all ran down the hill into the darkness.

Patric and Éclair stood together in the moonlight, panting. It was over. Patric was so happy he wanted to dance, but he felt too tired. He stood swaying with his head close to the ground. His nostrils flared, and his sides heaved. His heart was pounding. Sweat dripped from his coat to the frozen ground.

"There they go," said Éclair, gulping air as she watched them slink away. "Cowards all. So many against only one. But the night is cold, and they are so very hungry," she murmured. "Now, what is in this tree, I wonder?" She stood upright, balancing on her hind legs underneath the branch where Harry was hiding, and sniffed and sniffed the air. "There's a rabbit in this tree," she exclaimed. "Hmmmm, I love rabbit. Is this rabbit your friend?"

There was a sudden movement behind her, and she turned to find Patric very close. His ears were pinned back to the side of his head, and he said in a very quiet voice, "I am Patric the pony, and this rabbit is a friend of mine."

"Oh, now I understand" said Éclair, moving away hastily. Then, standing with her head held high, she said, "I am named Éclair, the Flash of Lightning. I am Éclair, the borzoi, the hunter of coyotes and rabbits, but I give you my word, your rabbit friend will always be safe with me."

Then Éclair ran in a circle, sniffing the ground, and as she ran she said, "You are a very brave and clever pony to hide your friend in the tree." Quickly she rolled and rolled on the ground under the tree, and then she shook herself all over until dust and dirt flew into the air. "Now, you and the rabbit wait here," she said. "I'll make sure the coyotes have all gone all the way home." And with that she ran swiftly around the rock, looking into the pools of darkness, but there were no coyotes hiding there. Then she ran down the hill to the pond and through the marshy ground. Are any coyotes hiding here? she wondered.

She stopped and unfolded her ears until they stood straight up on her head. She listened, but all she could hear was the rustle of the leaves and the gurgle of the pond in the silence of the night. She looked with her far-seeing eyes into the shadows, but they could find no trace of movement. She smelled the ground with her black nose. She smelled the coyotes, but the scent was getting older; the coyotes were moving further away. She listened again, but all she could hear was silence. There were no coyotes here. They were gone. Then she heard them far, far away. "Yip, yip, yip," they sang sadly.

Patric stared as she ran back up the hill toward him. He had never seen such a creature. How swiftly she ran. There were white curls on top of her back, and as she ran, her long, white coat shone silver in the moonlight.

"They are far away now," she told him, "beyond the meadow and the pond."

Patric gave a big sigh of relief. The coyotes were gone. Harry was safe. "Thank you for helping us. Without your help…" He shivered. He didn't want to think about it. It was too horrible. His nostrils flared, and he took long, shuddering breaths.

Éclair understood. She knew what he was thinking. She reached up and touched the pony's nose with her nose and stood quietly beside him, exchanging breaths. She waited for him to be calm.

Suddenly, a voice broke the silence and the stillness. "Éclair, Éclair, where are you?" Patric and Éclair turned and looked. It came from behind the rock, over the fence.

"Uh oh!" said Éclair. The dog show. She had forgotten the dog show. She stood still in the moonlight and then began looking back over first one shoulder and then the other, twisting and turning, this way and that, trying to see her coat. She said hurriedly, "I'm going to a dog show tomorrow. I am still beautiful, aren't I? I try to stay beautiful, but sometimes I forget, and then I get dirty and then I get into trouble."

"Yes," said Patric. "You are beautiful."

Éclair had mud from the marshy ground on her feet, and on her back there was dirt and grass from rolling. There was blood drying on a hind leg from where one of the coyotes had bitten her, and her long, white tail that reached all the way to the ground was covered in dry leaves, but it didn't matter. It didn't matter at all.

"You are beautiful, and brave too," he said.

Éclair looked at him with shining eyes and waggled her long, white tail from side to side. To and fro it went. To and fro. To and fro. Patric knew she was pleased.

"My owner doesn't know I can jump the fence, but I'll be watching out for you and your rabbit friend," she said, taking one last look down the hill. "Look at all the lights." The house lights and the barn lights had been turned on; even the lights along the driveway were shining brightly. People with flashlights were walking up the hill toward them. "Your family is coming for you. I must go now. I like to go to dog shows, but most of all I like to run very fast."

Patric watched her as she trotted up to the fence. "We will run together, pony, you and I," she said, and then she sprang easily over the fence and disappeared from his sight.

The pony stood silently. He shook himself all over. He was thinking about Harry. Perhaps we will run together, he thought, one day. He felt very cold and thirsty, and his side and the back of his hind legs hurt where the coyotes had bitten him. He walked slowly over to the tree and called out, "Harry, Harry, are you okay?"

Hidden in the highest part of the lowest branch among the leaves, Harry raised his head and opened his eyes. That was Patric's voice calling him. He heard the okay word. He was still alive; he was alive! He was so glad to be alive, but his voice was squeaky. "Are you okay, Patric?"

"I'm okay, thanks to Éclair," said Patric. "It's safe. You can jump down now." He stood under the branch where the rabbit was hiding. The rabbit jumped down from the branch and onto his back, and then Patric dropped stiffly to his knees so that Harry could jump to the ground. Harry scrambled down, but he was still afraid. He stood up on his hind legs. His long ears twisted this way and that. He looked and he listened all around him. He was ready to run.

"Are the coyotes gone?" asked Harry. "They ate all my brothers and sisters." He was trembling, and his nose twitched as he looked at Patric's side and throat.

"Yes, the coyotes have gone," said Patric. "We are safe now, Harry. Éclair, the white borzoi, is watching out for us—and, look, my family is coming." He pricked up his ears. He could hear little Jacob calling his name.

"Everyone watches out for rabbits," said Harry quietly, looking at Patric with his large, dark eyes, "in their own way. You are my very special friend. You saved my life."

"You will always be my special friend too," said Patric. "It's good to have friends," and he rubbed his nose gently against Harry's long ears.

Then slowly, with Harry beside him, Patric walked down the hill in the darkness toward the sound of the voices and the flashes of light. He was thinking about Froggy. "Now that was an adventure!" he said.